SYNCOPATED BLUE

SYNCOPATED BLUE

SYNCOPATED BLUE

SYNCOPATED BLUE

SYNCOPATED BLUE

SYNCOPATED BLUE

SYNCOPATED BLUE

SYNCOPATED BLUE

SYNCOPATED BLUE

SYNCOPATED BLUE

RYAN HENNESSY

—

Gill Books

Gill Books
Hume Avenue
Park West
Dublin 12
www.gillbooks.ie

Gill Books is an imprint of M.H. Gill and Co.

© Ryan Hennessy 2021
9780717191840

Compiled by Tony Clayton-Lea
Designed by Graham Thew
Illustrations by Megan Luddy
Printed by Hussar Books, Poland

This book is typeset in 9.5 on 12.5 Freight Text.
The paper used in this book comes from the wood pulp of
managed forests. For every tree felled, at least one tree is
planted, thereby renewing natural resources.

A CIP catalogue record for this book is available
from the British Library.
5 4 3 2 1

I began writing poetry around the age of 7 because my
father did it and his father before him too. I am so glad this
inherited expression has culminated in the publishing of my
first book of poetry.

I felt it would be remiss of me to do this book without
acknowledging the great man who inspired me then and
inspires me now.

So I would like to start the book with a poem written by
my father:

As I walk homewards on this sharp September night,
I watch the silent moon-rays skip from roof to roof,
Revealing chipped slates, and dormant moss, and probing insects.
Only the radar sound of the dark infamous bat disturbs the tranquil air.
Then I see the moonlit roof of the old school, the colosseum for dancers,
Where I danced my first shy dance, in that crippled old hall.
I think of that first wondrous night when I shyly swayed in rhythm,
And imagined that all eyes were on my clumsy feet.
There that building withers away to the soil all quiet and still,
Virtually razed by age and wind and rain.
But Rollermania, Discomania and Rock 'n' Roll lives on, silently,
And the ghosts of my dance and companions remain,
Amidst the clinging ivy and smothering cobwebs.

I

i'm jealous of the ivory
that her fingers gently touch
i wish i could be them
and damn i wish that could be us
her voice is soft as snowfall
and she doesn't have a clue
how i like to watch her playing
in her syncopated blue.

pint drinker
poetic thinker
one of the lads
pet to the teacher.
chocolatey gaze
can talk shit for days
sharp London tongue
of which i'd like to taste.

she's a lovely bunch of people
proper rock n roll
ink upon a needle
it's tattooed on her soul.

she's a connoisseur of evenings
a lighter-up of rooms
a bottler-up of feelings
a canvas for a bruise.

she's a talker without speaking
words fall from her eyes
a rush that's never leaving
the highest high of highs.

she's the champagne on the ceiling
the smoke under the door
she's the only living breathing
piece of heaven i'd die for.

first romances
second chances
sun kissed skin
and
awkward dances

trembling hands
and trembling lips
in the trembling lives
of trembling kids

broken bones
borrowed clothes
stealing kisses
and
skimming stones

abandoned bikes
and abandoned promise
in abandoned houses
we abandoned solace.

she sat cross legged
'cross the table
cross examining every millimetre of my
face.
wine in one hand, me in the other.

and her dress didn't sparkle
half as much as her eyes did
re-emerging every second
from the clasp of her eyelids
in a room full of people
she made it feel silent.
wildness, wildness.

there's an unwritten rule
between her and me
an unspoken tension
that only we can see
i'm unsure about it
and it's unsure of me
and this is un-how i thought
i would spend New Year's Eve.

and it was a peculiar thing
because we kissed
as if we missed each other
even though we had only just met.

i cannot relate to the words you speak
because unlike them
i would never leave your lips.

as i kissed her i felt the whole world
fall down around us.
i guess she had apoca-lips.

i don't mind you getting pissed
and rooting through your bag
of bar receipts and random shit
from blurry nights you've had.

i don't mind your sun-dried lips
not stopping for a yawn
mid-sentence when they should be still
they seem to carry on.

i don't mind the way you quip
that sometimes i'm not funny
because my skin is way too thick
to be bitten by you, honey.

i don't mind the crucifix
around your neck you wear
or the sonnet one-one-six
on your skin that you bare.

i don't mind how dark jokes slip
and from your mouth do fall
and i don't try to babysit 'cause
i don't mind at all.

we both can't sleep at night
but we could sleep atop a footpath
i don't know if it's our minds
or if we're both just fucking scumbags
but i'll talk to you till light
because i love your fucking comebacks.

"i'm outside."

i drop my phone and run to the front gate.

i open it and revealed to me are your teary
eyes and trembling voice.   17

"can i stay with you tonight?"

"of course you can, c'mere."

relight your cigarette as many times as
you want.
stop saying sorry because you don't want
to have sex tonight
i know it's too soon, i told you i'll wait.
you're not a bad person you're a good one
with a conscience.
yes, you can stay with me tonight and yes
we can go to bed now
and yes i'll turn off the light
i know it's early days but you don't have to
ask these questions
and you don't have to say you're sorry for
saying sorry.
it's so clichéd but i'm not like the men
before me.
your skin will never bruise again and
your words won't fall away
and if you really love it here so much
you can come here every day.
now kiss me one last time before i wake
up to you singing
and you can sleep upon my chest for just
as long as i am living.

in a world full of people who are
more than willing to display their talents
and lend their voices

in acts of defiant self-indulgence
it was the reluctance in her voice
that caused her soft song
to ring the loudest.

flowers in a supermarket are a moment of
beautiful relief in an otherwise mundane
and lifeless space.

so if the world is a supermarket then you
are my £5 flowers.

i hail from a town called Athy
once mentioned in a Kavanagh poem.
some people would call it a dive
but i would call it 'home'.

nobody will ever quite understand
the feeling that pours over my body
and into my soul as i stand beneath
these Bermuda Triangle trees
and gaze upwards to the heavens
as the raindrops filter down
through the semi-dormant leaves.
leaves half asleep, half dancing,
the wind unsure whether to
provoke them or let them rest.
i see the wind as a reflection of myself.
as the tiny droplets permeate my skin
and flood my inner recesses, i wonder
has anyone else ever taken such pleasure
from something so simplistic?
or is it i alone who finds refuge in the raindrops?

i woke up this morning and i cursed myself
because i had fallen even deeper for you
again.
that's the 65th day in a row.
i thought we were supposed to be taking
things slow.

the soles of your feet pressed against my
bare chest
i lift them and press them against my lips
instead
you smile with a makeup-less face
your legs split and allow me to fall into
place
i can feel your warmth on my thighs
your eyes alive and inches from mine
"please" you say
i was never one not to oblige.

you're in my room in my head so much
that you should start paying rent here
at least once a month.   27

28   if you are my lover, please skip this poem.

i had the buzzer for the gate fixed a few
weeks ago
but i still haven't told you
because i love walking out to meet you
and accepting your half nervous, half
excited laugh
with an arms over the shoulders embrace
and a kiss to the forehead.
i just cannot give up that short, hand
entwined walk back to the front door
together.

i promise that this is the only thing i'll ever
keep from you.

i make you laugh
you make me cum
i take your hand
you take my lungs

i tell you things
you tell me off
i let you sing
you let me talk

i breathe you in
you breathe me out
i kiss your chin
you kiss my mouth

i stroke your hair
you stroke my mind
i say i'm near
you say you're mine

i touch your feet
you touch my neck
i fail to sleep
you fail to check

      i fuck you slow
      you fuck on top
      i say i'm close
      you say don't stop

            i hold you tight
            you hold me too
            i find your eyes
            you find my blue

                  we lose ourselves
                  we've come to find
                  i need your help
                  and you need mine.

i woke up 15 times during the night
because waking up to you
is my favourite sight.

this heart of mine was opened against my will
and thrust into my stomach at 100 miles per hour.
just one look makes my belly feel like it's made from stars.
like there's galaxies floating through my veins that only her
and i know about.
and the unspoken words mean the most.
the words we both want to say but aren't brave enough to let
out. maybe one day we will.
at night she wanders into my dreams. so mischievously, so
elegantly. and treads across my heart until i wake.
i think i've escaped her presence in my mind until i spend the
day thinking about her. wondering if she's thinking about me.
wondering if her body longs for mine like mine longs for
hers.
i'll learn how to swim if that's what it takes, fuck i'll even
learn how to fly.
just to be on the receiving end of her extended gaze. the one
that lasts longer than anybody else's.

i wanna get lost in those eyes.
lost in those conversations.
lost in her laugh.
lost in her stories.
lost in her city.
lost in her.

are we gonna talk
or watch this stupid tv show?

you strolled in in stripes
not wanting to fight but to listen.

i feel like two different people.
you tell me you can handle them both.

i reveal to you hand-picked flowers
as a silver lining to my passive aggression.

you remove the string from the stems
and tie it around our wrists.

in binding us together you removed
every ounce of worry my brain had found.

Christmas doesn't seem so cold now
that you have talked me down.

this isn't even a poem it's just two lines
spaced out and out.

i mean, i only started rhyming the couplets
on the Christmas line somehow.

anyway, i'm losing my trail of thought
just like you do mid-sentence.

and you miss the time we drank mulled wine
in Camden, so pretentious.

but we'll share more times and drink more wine
and look back and miss those too.

and for as long as you want and for
as long as i can, i'll take care of you.

when you're not here
it's weird.

it feels like the house misses you.

Michael's hats ain't selling
brutal lack of weddings
but Lucy loved his stand
and left with hat in hand
an act of warmth so telling.

i love the chaos that you leave behind
in this room in this house in this heart of
mine.

II

tried to find a part
that wasn't slightly pretty.
failed from head to toe.

you're my favourite atomic collection
and of them i know a few
but none that get the attention
that my neck hairs give to you

you're my favourite contradiction
and i'll never understand
how you feel like an affliction
that i'm so glad i had.

i wish my life were as boring as that of the
two men
who stood outside the hotel,
appalled because we were young and
beautiful
and both wearing leopard-print coats.

your knees met the cold tile.
you looked into the mirror with that
apologetic expression i've become so familiar
with.
the mirror looked at me and i returned the favour.
it would've been easy for you to turn around and
cut out the middle man but i knew you were too
afraid to do that.
we half exchanged some words and i turned on
my heels to the bedroom.
you followed soon after and we lay on
the bed.
a brief silence and darting back and forth of
eyes occurred between us.

"why did you leave the bathroom like that?" says
you

"because i know you're keeping something from
me," says i.

you knew why i had left like that and i knew that
you would follow. so our exchanging of words
was rendered obsolete.
i did what i always do and remained silent in
hope that it would break you and it did.
you unplugged your consciousness and spilled
everything you had been holding back into the
space between us.
i pulled your body towards me like a wave
picking up a shipwreck's debris and i listened to
every word.
i knew that my ears were the first that these
words were falling upon and i reacted with a
reciprocal stroking of your spine and holding of
your head.

i didn't say much because i knew i didn't have to,
you just needed me to listen.
and i did until your mouth became lazier along
with your eyes and they both fell asleep with you.
i lay awake with your words for a while and got to
know them. i carry them with me still and they
hold a great weight.

but there's comfort in knowing you're walking
around a few philosophical pounds lighter.

i tried and i tried not to fall in love with
every little molecule, every compartment
of every little part of you
i fall apart when i see it

maybe i will change my mind
'cause i always do that sometimes

darlin', i'm falling
for the hundredth thousandth time
since you acquaint your lips with mine
darlin', i'm falling
falling in slow motion
right into your ocean.

if i could have one superpower i would not
want to fly or teleport or travel back in time.

i would simply want the power to let you
into my mind so that you could see
yourself through my lens.

and feel the unashamed love and desire
that pulses though my body when you
stand before me.

you sat on top of me and we argued.
your hair pulled back how i like it, revealing those
hypnotic pools that laymen refer to as "eyes".
i spoke of insecurities and insignificance and
how they might become debilitating for us.
you were so sure they wouldn't.
in fact you were so sure it was as if you had seen
the inside of my skull for yourself.
i contested the words that stumbled from your
lips.
all of this back and forward. it was dizzying.
you posed a question to me and
then all of a sudden everything
moved
out
of
the
way.

and the words spilled from my mouth

"because i love you."

you became sickly
and we joked that it was because i had
told you i loved you for the very first time.
your pale complexion pressed against
my neck as i carried you to the bedroom
and spilled you onto the bed like a newborn.
in tandem we de-burdened your frame of its
clothing as to alleviate the feverish warmth.
i placed you gently beneath the covers and
placed myself gently beside you.
you pleaded with me to stop making you laugh
because you were afraid it would make you
throw up.
the helplessness i felt was that of frustration but
also of enlightenment.
of course i knew i cared about you. for god's sake
i had just confessed my love for you.
but as i pressed my chest to your back
and lips to your cheekbone
i realised i was longing
for your illness to be removed
from your body and transported to mine.
i, then, as a man who grossly detests any sort of
sickly feeling knew that the words i had delivered
to you earlier in the evening were in their truest
form.
you fell asleep and i laughed and conceded to
the universe.
what a brilliantly sick joke it had played on me.

16-year-old me would be really happy with where he ended up. Well, once the Prozac wore off.

i hate those "don't you worry" poems
those "you will never be alone"s
those empty words and empty quotes
i won't have that for you.

and i won't be right every time
i'll probably even cross a line
but all those negatives are mine
i won't have that for you.

and some people will love to hate
and use your name as drama bait
yet even when you wind me up 'til late
i won't have that for you.

i guess the sentiment of this
is i love your senti-mentalness
and sometimes i have a problem listening
but i won't have that for you.

i cannot quite pinpoint the exact moment
where i knew that i loved you.

but i knew that you loved me when you
said "i miss you" because i was facing the
other way to watch the tv.

i go gently as to not wake you from your
sleep
pleading with the boards beneath the
door for not to creak
the print from sheet and pillow has been
borrowed by my cheek
tired from the naked night and kissing of
your feet
i leave the quiet of your door and fall on to
the street
call me when you wake my love and tell
me of your dreams

i'm so glad that you exist
at the same time that i do
i could never cease this love
and believe me i have tried to.

reach into my chest and take my heart
before you leave
'cause since the day we met it has not
belonged to me

you're only 4,828.3 miles away

and it's only been 876,581.277 minutes

since I last saw you

but who's counting?

i lie on the bed grasping the stone you
gave me
and imagine your aeroplane passing by
my window.
imagine if through the clouds you could
see me
and through the stone you could feel me.
to everybody else i know these thoughts
would seem impossible
but i know that you are sitting in 25B
thinking the same thing
and that's all that matters to me.

i hate London when it steals you from me
and i hate the plane that brought you there.
i hate the man that checked your ticket and said
it was okay.
i hate the train that carried you from Heathrow to
your apartment without a question.
i hate your job, though it's the same as mine,
because it takes you from me when i least expect
it.
i hate your landlord for leaving out the keys so
that you could be one more door further away
from me.
i hate your mother for creating you in the perfect
way that she did.
i hate the space that sleeps beside you in my
absence and breathes your essence in.
i hate the ringing of my phone because it's a
reminder that you're not here to speak in person.
i hate every single piece of every single mile and
every single wave of every single ocean.
and every time i close my eyes i hate it when
they open.
i hate myself i hate my hand when it's not yours
that it's holding.

and i hate the way i hate these things
and hate these things i do
and the funny, fucked, amazing thing
is it's because i love you.

probably should hang up
right now but
instead i nod my head.
novels from her own half life
coming from her
English bed.
should have said goodbye but i
said "carry on" instead.

my heart is in Hampstead
and i can't live without it.
God, i hope that she found it
and put her rib cage around it.
my heart is in Hampstead.

i read you poems through the phone
as you're drifting off to sleep
grasping the supermarket teddy
i had bought you just last week.

i try to keep my speaking soft
so that your eyes can rest
but when i say a line you love
i hear your gentle breath.

i mark the corner of a page
if the words feel just like you
like the mention of a nervous laugh
or of the colour blue.

i want my words to fall away
and land inside your dreams
and keep you warm and kiss your head
and soften all your sheets.

i'll see you soon and hold you soon
and read you poems in skin
and calm your head and kiss your neck
and breathe your beauty in.

came down from the air

with nothing to declare

except my love for you.

my suit doesn't travel well.
much like Guinness, or an Irish
grandmother to an equatorial climate.
it creases like paper in the hand of a
disgruntled schoolboy, so i leave it at home.
much like we should with Guinness, or an
Irish grandmother when travelling to an
equatorial climate.

is there water in an ocean
that's a different shade of blue
than the one that i grew up with
in my head?
is there something in existence
that's more beautiful than you?
'cause if there is well then
i haven't seen it yet.

a bird ricochets in the wind of the Dublin
distance.
a hotel window and a couple of miles is all
that separates him and us.
he is unaware that i am watching him and
you are unaware that i am listening to you.
nonsensical words spill from your mind in
my peripheral and fall onto my chest just
beside your head.
my left arm holds your weight while my
right arm searches for your hair.
they both know that in a couple of hours
we have to leave and they hate it as much
as we do.
because this is home. a hotel room or a
queue for a store or a frantic street of
people. wherever you are, as long as it's
with me, it is home.
and here we are in this bed acting as if the
world is ending and we will never see each
other again.
but much like the bird that ricochets
we will return home safely once the wind
dies down.

when the lights are dim
and the sheets are calling
it's you that i want to see.
when i'm lost within
and i can't stop falling
i want you here with me.
when it's cold outside
and my bones are shaking
i'll look to you for heat.
when i run and hide
and can't help escaping
it's you i long to meet.
when my body aches
and my heart is craving
you will be the cause.
when i make mistakes
that are gone past saving
my breath for you will pause.
when my eyes are rested
and my mind alert
i will wander to your door.
when my love is tested
by all your hurt
i will beg you give me more.

you wake me with a kiss
and i one-eyed look at you
so beautiful like this
more beautiful through two

on 14th Street
Sofia goes to flower school
and her parents are divorced
but they're still cool.
in her yellow glasses
and her Louis boots
tread softly on my heart
'cause it's still blue.

and i'll kiss her feet forever
if she wants me to
and i'll always write her letters
in the afternoon

Sofia has my heart and
she paints it like it's art in
a Parisian garden
and i watch her dance in silhouette
in her New York apartment.
the sunlight tells the morning
to wake me with a yawn and
i watch her light a cigarette.

Sofia has my heart.

IV

beneath your eyes
the colour of dead rose petals forms
and invites me in unwillingly.

it broke my heart when you asked if i thought you were
pretty

because i knew you were not used to hearing it.

and it broke my heart when you asked if i would hold you
after sex

because i knew you were not used to feeling it.

it broke my heart when you asked me if i hug my mother
often

because i knew you were not used to doing it.

and it broke my heart when you asked me if i would tell my
friends about you

because i knew you were so used to hiding it.

in times when my hands are idle
they tend to apply a ferocious grip
around my trachea that cuts off
the flow of happiness between
my heart and my mind.
utter carnage ensues.

there is a sea of blood where
the tiny arcs of joy used to sail
to and fro. the arcs are now nothing
more than ruins, remains, protruding from
the wasteland that they once danced
upon. alas, when something or anything
is placed unto my hands, the self-built
dam is self-destroyed.

the voyage resumes, there are arcs with
wind in their sails once more.
although they are not arcs of happiness
but arcs of occupation, they are still
greater than the arcs of self-hate.
so much greater that they rule the sea now.
for a while at least.

i sat there in a funereal state.
my father had told me that my mother's
mother was going to die.
i was almost immediately transported
back to her soft hands, as they tilted my
head backwards in order to pour water
over my head.
she told me the water would not get in my
eyes then; she knew i was afraid.
but now she is the reason that there is
water in my eyes.
i will no longer have her soft hands here to
protect me from the stinging, from the
seeing, from the crying.
Elizabeth my dear; i'm sorry that you're dying.

i'm sure behind the weed smoke

the D10s

the amphetamines

the lager

the childhood trauma

the identity issues

the punches to the face

the reckless driving

the attention seeking

the lying cheating stealing

the birthday party ruining

the scene causing

the family disappointing

there's a nice person in there somewhere.
i'm just sorry i never met them.

have you ever felt like an acceptance
speech in the pocket of a loser's
jacket?

note to 23-year-old me:

breaking someone else won't fix yourself.

the trash-lined streets of Portobello
guide us on our way
not knowing where we're going
but too afraid to say.

your head upon my shoulder
with hair that's freshly dyed
we sat upon your front step
where i spoke and you cried.

we hail a cab to somewhere
that you don't want to go
i leave you with reluctance
and brand new clothes in tow.

we'll meet again tonight
having spent the day with words
and i hope you keep me some
even if they're ones that hurt.

the first time you came into my room
we sat nervously on either side of the bed
both afraid to make the first move.

the last time you came into my room
we sat nervously on either side of the bed
both afraid to make the last move.

i don't want
anyone else
and neither does
she.
the problem is
i'm talking about
her but she's
not talking about
me.

the skies told the streetlights to guide me home, as they could no longer look after me. it was their time to sleep. in their absence the wind came and toyed with my coat tails and made my eyes even more teary than they already were.

i've walked this path a thousand times, from her door to my door and back again, but this would be the last time. this would be the last time because i grew incapable of loving her, of loving anybody. including myself.

her smell was still borrowed by my skin from that final embrace and i could still taste the salt from her tears. i imagined her in her room, whimpering like it was the end of the world. then i imagined myself running all the way back to see her and, before you knew it, growing incapable of loving her again.

on that final walk home, as the lights inconsistently painted my face orange, and the pain and trauma of what had just occurred painted my soul black, i knew. i knew that someone somewhere would cut right across this path and onto her door, and they would grow capable of loving her how she should be loved, relentlessly, forever.

she had such a profound effect on my
heart that i now use her as a mark of time.
life before her, and life after her.

do you know how debilitating it is when
cold weather reminds you of someone?

as soon as the winter breeze hits my
body i am instantly transported to your
door.

i wrote some words about you again today
and i tore them up
and let the wind take them from my hands
and give them to the sea
because keeping them to myself
was once good enough
but now even i can't bear to read.

i wondered had i faded into the frames of
famous faces in the corner.

or was i illuminated, nervously
emancipated by the thought of

a possible embrace impossible for me to
trace if that's in order.

i hate my hesitating – now i'll always be left
waiting here in wonder.

i am a man in women's clothes
and nails that are perfectly painted.
i am a man who writes these poems
about how his heart couldn't take it.
i am a man who expresses himself
through whatever means he can find.
i am a man who talks to his friends
about what's going on inside.
i am a man who cries when he's sad
and shakes when his stomach does drop.
i am a man who is good and is bad
i am a man full stop.

it's better to have loved and lost than
to have not had anything.

and it's better to have lived at a cost,
there's not an arse in my pocket.

you know that i would give it all up just for
a night, just for another drink.

the only way you know that you had it is if
you lost it.

i wish you were

her(e).

as the wind swept across my windowsill it brought with it the rain's applause. i watched as it magnified and then deafened with each sweeping moment. beyond it were 52 dormant houses, some two storey, some one storey, but each with a story of its own.

one had windows painted black, and one had windows bursting into life every now and then with colour.

the houses didn't care about the rain, in the same way that i didn't care about the houses. they could all tumble down one by one to their foundations and i wouldn't even notice. for as my eyes were gazing out of the window, i was gazing into myself. we were working independently of one another.

and it was raining inside of me, too, flooding even. the difference was that the rain outside made my room feel snug and inviting and safe. but the rain inside made my room feel stark and cold and unfamiliar.

bar fight record of 5 and 0
heartbreak record is the opposite.

using my hands instead of my heart
is the reason for both of those things.

if a psychiatrist only has himself to talk to
then isn't he the crazy one?

v

mo ghrá agus mo chroí

both belong to thee.

she's lost. but lost like torrential rain would be on the dusty
surface of the African plains.

she doesn't know it yet but she needs to get lost to the point
of desertion. because now she's only half lost. that's why she
accepts half love. half love and half words and half sex. from
a person that once fully loved her.

until she reaches the point of pure unforgiving loss, only
then will she see that she's worth more than she is currently
being valued.

and i'll pick her up and dust her off like an old record. and i'll
put the needle to her surface and watch her spin and allow
her to sing again. but this time she won't be a background
noise. she'll be the soundtrack to my movie and i'll be the
soundtrack to hers.

and what was once grey will be technicolour
and what was once frightening will be exhilarating
and what was once guilt will be reward
and what was once a fight will be a joke
and what was once trembling lips will be kissed lips
and what was once an idle mind will be a nurtured one
and what was once an early morning will be a sunrise
and what was once inescapable will be merely a memory
and through all of this, my love
what was once you
will be you again.

nimble brown eyes gaze carefully
wanting nothing but to love and be loved.
species of yours or of mine,
it matters not to me.
an overwhelming effervescence i behold.
for the kinetic. for the inanimate.
for what lives and guides.
for what never lived and never guided.

reconvening with your eyes
more beautiful than London skies
the leg on which your coffee lies
is what i'm jealous of.

reuniting with your smile
i haven't felt it in a while
you make my stomach run a mile
that's all you're guilty of.

your hair still holding Suffolk sand
the way it used to hold my hand
we spoke of skin devoid of tan
just how we would before.

and i've never tried to understand
why souls connect or feelings land
but your name is spilled and stained and stands
all over my heart's floor.

"Cailín"

stroke my spine until i'm sleeping
bring me to my knees with your kiss
in the darkest nights come creeping
tell me everything you've missed.
hold me till my ribs are broken
tighter than anyone could know
throw me out into the open
my body can't feel the snow.
hurt me with your eyes, impale me,
that's all that i've ever asked
kill me with your lies and fail me
i'm numb, my pain is masked.
tease me with your presence then leave me
with a hole that does not end
cut me scar me bleed me
i'm the master of pretend.

for a moment all i knew was your body
i could see no further than your skin
nothing else existed
just you. and i within.
i drowned in those green pools
that flowed between your eyelids
not wanting to be saved
for it was beautiful, not violent.
your lips moved all around me
your breath would never tire
one movement of your hips
would set my soul on fire.
your grip said "never let me go"
"i belong in this very place"
my hands they reassured you
my lips fell on your face.
i'll stop loving you
when birds no longer fly
when leaves don't change with the season
when the oceans' waves turn dry.

i use the birthmark on her back
as my point of reference in the darkness.

there is no other warmth like the
middle of the night
through semi woke eyes
bare skinned
warmth of your body.

to be loved by you is to be imitated by you.
footsteps matched with footsteps and trouser
legs rolled the same.

to be loved by you is to be held by you.
and i mean held in its strongest form, your arms
like vice grips hugging until i bruise.

to be loved by you is to be observed by you.
through the corner of my eye i feel you taking in
every one of my brush strokes as if i am a
fixture at the Louvre.

to be loved by you is to be spoken of by you.
my ears burn when we are apart because i know
some poor innocent bystander is learning my
name and my nature unwillingly.

to be loved by you is to be told by you.
you were eager to distinguish between "i love
you" and "i am in love with you". you needed me
to know it was the latter of the two.

to be loved by you is to be touched by you.
you touch me as if i am the rarest, most ancient
artefact ever discovered.

to be loved by you is to be woken by you.
your eyes wide and transfixed as if i had just fallen
to earth and right into your bed.

to be loved by you is to be laughed at by you.
with every eyes-closed, face to the ceiling cry of
joy i feel another stitch binding our hearts
together.

to be loved by you is to be blessed by you.
i owe a thousand lifetimes to whoever gave you
your heart and allowed it to love me.
because to be loved by you is the truest,
most unspeakable, unfathomable pleasure that i have
ever felt coursing through my veins.

to be loved by you is everything.

we passed a flightless ladybird
between our hands as we sat
on the windowsill.
our rusting jewellery would clash from
time to time and intensify the tension
that danced between our bodies.
i asked what material your trousers
were made from as an excuse
to touch your leg.
a sad girl sang a sad song in the speaker but it
soaked into the walls.
there was nothing that we could absorb but one
another.
i pointed towards the distant streetlight
shrouded in rainfall.
you stared in awe at it and i stared in awe at you.

that night we too would be shrouded in rainfall.
in a children's playground we silently toyed with
the idea of one another.
our hands would linger slightly longer every time
we touched.
until, by the tyre swing we traded the smelling of
one another's hair and as i removed my nose
from your scalp we fell into each other's eyes
and kissed like our lives depended on it.
it was a kiss that felt like it was never going to
end.
and i don't think it ever did.

we both have a debilitating fear of getting
old
but at least we're in it together.

i can't wait to grow middle aged with you.

they say we don't live forever
and i guess they're kinda right
but i think we live forever
in what we leave behind.

sometimes i think i'm an eejit
and sometimes i think i'm a genius
sometimes i think i believe in
some kind of version of Jesus
somehow i thought that by leaving
her i would forget my feelings.
somebody tell me to breathe in.
i mean out.
somebody tell me to leave it
and lie down.
and i won't drown.

and stop being so scared of everything
that's a waste of life
and you don't hate that girl
she's actually kind of nice.
you're just upset that she mocked
the shirt you were wearing that night.
forget it.

and i'm talking to you, well i'm talking to me.
but we're all the same, aren't we?
and as this new decade beckons us forward
let's step into it wholeheartedly
and say things with our chest
and say things we'll regret

but say them! and feel them and be them.
give yourself love and give your life reason.
i mean it! i mean it!

embrace pain and heartache and stress and fear
and love and laughter and sex and cheer.
and have a happy life.
and a happy new year.

young men, take the pen and put it to the
page.
young men, wear the clothes that people
think are strange.
young men, share your thoughts, i promise
they'll be heard.
young men, kiss the boys, the others and
the girls.
young men, tell your friends and tell your
family too,

that you'll be there for them and ask if
they'll be there for you.
young men, be the version of yourselves
you love
and own up to the feelings that you feel
you're guilty of.
'cause you cannot be guilty if you live your
life as free.
young men, go and be who you were born
to be.

please remember

people who do not accept others for who
they are, have not yet accepted
themselves.

i'm at the end of every call
and every room of every hall
and every ledge to catch your fall
i'm at the end for you.

i'm at the end of every tear
and every month and every year
and when you think you'll disappear
i'm at the end for you.

i'm at the end of every day
and every cab ride every way
and every time you'll hear me say
i'm at the end for you.

i'm at the end of every sleep
and every mother induced weep
and every void that feels too deep
i'm at the end for you.

i copy your breath when we're falling
asleep
because the mere thought of us being out
of sync
chills me to my bones.
and you copy my walk when we're out on
the street
because the mere thought of us being out
of sync
makes you feel alone.
and it's funny how we hate this
syncopation like we do
when it's the reason that i went
and named this whole book after you.